Tip it
Tap it

Written by Abbie Rushton
Illustrated by Natalia Moore

Collins

sit

sip

pips

tip

pat pat

pat pat

tap tap

8

tap tap

a pit

tip in

a tap

pat pat

/s/

After reading

Letters and Sounds: Phase 2

Word count: 20

Focus phonemes: /s/ /a/ /t/ /p/ /i/ /n/

Curriculum links: Understanding the World

Early learning goals: Reading: use phonic knowledge to decode regular words and read them aloud accurately

Developing fluency

- Your child may enjoy hearing you read the book.
- Read with expression to encourage your child to do the same, e.g. on page 4, read **pips** with surprise.

Phonic practice

- Turn to page 2. Ask your child to sound out the letters in the word, then blend. (s/i/t – **sit**) Repeat for page 6. (p/a/t – **pat**)
- On pages 4 and 5, ask your child to sound out **pips** and **tip**. Can they spot which letter sounds are the same in both words?
- Look at the "I spy sounds" pages (14–15). Point to the sun, and say "sun", emphasising the /s/ sound. Ask your child to find more things that start with the /s/ sound. (*sand, sea, sunhat, strawberries, sun cream, shade, sauce, sandwiches, seagull, spade, surfer*)

Extending vocabulary

- Take turns to read and mime the action on pages 2, 3, 5, 6, 7, 8, 9, 11 and 13. You can then mime and mouth a word, and ask your child to guess what it is.